Looking for Dad

ELLEN FRANCES

Illustrated by Annie White

 sundance

Copyright © 1999 Sundance Publishing

Published by
Sundance Publishing
234 Taylor Street
Littleton, MA 01460

Copyright © text Ellen Frances
Copyright © illustrations Annie White
Project commissioned and managed by
Lorraine Bambrough-Kelly, The Writer's Style
Designed by Cath Lindsey/design rescue

First published 1998 by
Addison Wesley Longman Australia Pty Limited
95 Coventry Street
South Melbourne 3205 Australia
Exclusive United States Distribution: Sundance Publishing

ISBN 0-7608-3292-7

Printed In Canada

Contents

CHAPTER 1

Missing Mom

John was feeling lonely. His mom was getting married, and everyone was happy about it. Everyone except John.

John liked living with Mom. They never needed anyone else, until she met Steve. Now, Mom said she needed Steve, too.

Mom was never home! She was busy at work, busy with housework, or busy going out—with Steve.

John didn't need Steve! John didn't want Steve! John wanted Mom all to himself.

John had to spend a lot of time with the babysitter. He didn't like the babysitter. She watched too much TV and spent too much time talking to her boyfriend on the phone.

She didn't like throwing a football like his mom did.

And she said John had to stay in his room and read.

CHAPTER 2

A Plan Is Hatched

John tried to figure out how to make Mom stay home. He tried keeping his room clean, but that didn't keep Mom home.

He tried taking her breakfast in bed, but that didn't keep her home.

It just made her late for work because it took half an hour to brush the toast crumbs off the sheets after they had a food fight!

He even tried to help Mom with the food shopping. But after he dropped a box of eggs,

knocked over a pile of cans,

and fell into the freezer when he tried to
get the frozen peas,

Mom said he better stay home from now
on.

One day, Steve came to their house for dinner. John said he had a stomachache and went to bed.

Another day, Steve came to take them to a movie, but John hid outside. His mom thought maybe he'd gone to a friend's house to play.

John could hear everything his mom and Steve were saying. They were talking about their wedding.

John stomped off and kicked a hole in his clubhouse wall.

CHAPTER 3

The Wedding Day

And now the awful day had come.

John sat on the front steps gazing at a snail's trail that wound down the path. He was wearing new shoes, a new shirt, a new tie, and a hot, stuffy suit. Everything was itchy.

John's mom and Steve were married in the backyard. Now everyone was inside the house eating, drinking, and talking. Lots of presents were stacked high on a table.

His mom looked nice. Steve didn't.

John didn't like Steve's fancy vest or his shiny blue shirt. And his trouser legs were too short! You could see his blue socks! John was embarrassed by Steve's appearance.

John had to live with this man from now on. He was sure Steve was going to be really bossy and grumpy—and John still didn't know what to call him! His mom said he should call Steve "Dad," but John didn't want to. Steve wasn't a "dad" sort of person.

"It's not fair," thought John. "She should have asked me if I wanted to marry him, too."

John couldn't remember his real dad, but he knew what a good dad would be like. He'd read about them in books and seen them on TV.

John picked up a stick and drew a picture of a good dad in the dirt. He gave his dad a long, bushy beard (to keep him warm when they played football with each other), a big, wobbly potbelly (to shield him from the wind when they were out fishing), and a smelly pipe (so he could tell if his dad was nearby).

Steve didn't smoke, shaved every day, and stayed thin because he liked to run in marathons.

"Steve's not right. He's not what I want. I'll have to find a dad on my own," thought John.

CHAPTER 4

Looking for Dad

John stood up and marched into the house. There were lots of people inside. He knew some of them. He was sure there must be a dad for him in there somewhere. He just needed to find the right one.

He looked around. He felt a bit scared, but he couldn't stop now. It was too important. So, pretending he was a spy on a secret mission, he started to look closely at the wedding guests.

Leaning against the fireplace was one of the biggest men he had ever seen! The man didn't have a pipe, and he didn't have a beard, but he did have a great fat, squishy-looking potbelly! It would be just right for snuggling into if he gave you a hug.

John waited politely until the man had stopped sipping his soft drink and talking to a pretty woman.

John thought he'd better be nice. It's a good idea to impress someone if you want him to be your dad.

He stood in front of the big potbelly and said in his most polite voice, "Excuse me, but I'm looking for a new dad, and you look just right. Do you like fishing, and would you please be my dad?"

The woman started giggling behind her hand, and the big man laughed so loudly that his fat belly jiggled wildly.

"Good grief!" he wheezed. "What on earth would I do with a son? And fishing! When would I have time to go fishing? I'm far too busy running the bank."

He laughed so loudly that people looked around to see who was making so much noise. They wondered if they should be laughing, too.

The man took an enormous purple handkerchief from his pocket and mopped his forehead. "Go away now, like a good boy, and let me enjoy myself."

A waiter walked by carrying a plate full of little sausages. The big-bellied bank manager grabbed a handful of sausages as the waiter passed. Then, turning his back on John, he started talking to the pretty woman again.

John was embarrassed. He felt as if everyone was laughing at him.

"How rude!" John thought. "That man might have a great wobbly, squishy, cuddly potbelly, but he didn't have to laugh at me. I wouldn't want him for my dad anyway."

John wandered around the room some more. None of the men he saw were what he was looking for.

He went upstairs. There were more people up there.

A man was sitting on the floor of the hallway, staring at a painting on the wall. He had a long, fluffy beard that flowed all the way to his waist. His hair was tied in a ponytail with a black ribbon.

John sat down beside him. The man kept staring at the painting.

"Excuse me," began John. The man didn't look at him.

"Pardon me," said John. "I'm looking for a new dad, and you'd be just about right. I was wondering if you play football. And would you be interested in being my dad?"

"Football," whispered the man. "Deep!"

John scratched his head and looked puzzled. He decided to try something else. Something easier.

"I like your beard," he said.

The man nodded. "Heavy!" he said.

John stood up and walked away. That man might have a great beard, but what good was a dad if you couldn't talk to him or understand anything he said?

John walked back downstairs. Mom was
laughing and joking with the guests. She
didn't see him go by.

John sighed. He was tired, and his shoes were hurting him. He walked through the kitchen. The cook was arguing with one of the waiters about some spilled sauce. A waitress was struggling with an expensive bottle of vinegar, trying to pull out its cork.

His uncle came into the kitchen and began looking in the cupboards for a bottle of antacid. He belched and winked at John. "Fancy food always does this to me," he said.

John went out the back door. Standing on the porch smoking a cigar, was the waiter.

The odor of the cigar filled the air as the waiter blew smoke rings. John thought, "Smoking is a bad idea, but you'd always know he was coming if he was your dad."

John stood beside the man, looked up at him, and said, "I need a dad. Are you a dad?"

The man pulled the cigar from his mouth, crouched down beside John, stared into his face, and said, "Nope! And I'm not aiming to be one either!"

Smoke covered John's face and went down his throat. The smell was horrible! John started coughing and spluttering.

The waiter stood up again and stuffed the cigar back in his mouth. "Now go away, kid," he said. "I'm not wasting my coffee break talking with a squirt like you."

CHAPTER 5

Nobody Loves Me

John jumped off the porch and ran to his
clubhouse. He shut himself inside.

His eyes stung, his feet hurt, and his whole body itched. He pulled off his new tie and stuffed it into his pocket. Nobody wanted to be his dad.

One by one, tears started trickling down his face. It wasn't fair!

Just then there was a knock on the clubhouse door. Steve was standing outside. He asked John if he could come in. John didn't say anything.

Steve squeezed inside anyway. He pulled a folded white handkerchief out of his shirt pocket and handed it to John.

"What's wrong?" he asked. "I saw you talking to those men. Did they say something that upset you?"

John shook his head. He didn't think anyone had seen. His mom had been too busy to notice.

Steve sat down beside him. "What were you talking about?"

John didn't want to tell him. Steve might get angry.

"You can tell me," said Steve. "I won't tell anyone. I promise."

John put his fingers over his eyes and peered out at Steve. He didn't look quite so big and bad when you looked at him this way!

"You'll get mad," said John.

"I promise I won't," said Steve.

"No matter what?" asked John.

"No matter what!" promised Steve.

So, little by little, John told Steve the whole story.

Steve nodded his head and listened. Every now and then, he asked a question. Then he listened again. He didn't mind talking to a kid.

"That's okay," said Steve, when John ran out of words.

"It is?" asked John.

Steve stood up and shook John's hand, "Allow me to introduce myself," he said. "I'm Steve Linden. I'm new around here, and I'm really a nice person when you get to know me. But I don't know many people in this neighborhood, and I'm scared that I'm going to do something stupid and make everybody laugh at me. You look like a nice person. Would you be my friend and tell me what to do to fit in?"

John nodded solemnly.

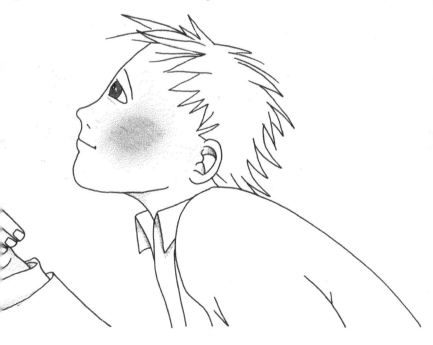

Steve sat down again.

"Good," he said. "After all, I don't want to get in trouble with your mom for doing the wrong thing!"

John started laughing. She could be grumpy, at times. He started telling Steve about their food fights and football games.

After a while, Steve left and went back to the house. He returned with a huge plate of hot sausages and barbecue sauce.

John could tell he was coming back because he could smell Steve's aftershave lotion as he walked across the yard.

They sat and ate and talked some more. Steve made jokes, and John laughed at his jokes.

Steve promised to take him fishing soon. He said he liked fishing. He even said he'd help John make his very own fishing rod.

There was another knock at the door. It was John's mom.

"Everyone's gone home," she said. "Is there room for one more in here?"

Mom was carrying a present. It was for John—a new football.

"We can throw it to each other," said Steve.

"Tomorrow," said Mom. "Now it's time for bed."

They all climbed out of the clubhouse.

"Want a ride?" asked Steve.

John climbed up on his back. Steve's arms felt strong and secure as they carried John into the house.

Steve bounced up the stairs and into John's bedroom. Then they went into the bathroom and brushed their teeth together. They shared John's green, sparkly toothpaste.

"Are you okay now?" asked Steve. "I was worried about you."

"Yep," said John, as he got into his pajamas. "Thanks . . . Dad."

And John's new dad proudly tucked him into bed.

About the Author

Ellen Frances

Ellen Frances likes to believe there are stories hiding everywhere, waiting to be discovered.

Originally from Melbourne, Australia, Ellen has taught school, from the elementary grades through high school.

Ellen has also worked as a jazz singer, storyteller, children's TV columnist, scriptwriter, journalist, photographer, and author.

Currently, she lives in the United States, and continues to explore new and different ways of telling a good story.

About the Illustrator

Annie White

Annie White's work has appeared on brochures, posters, stickers, and computer home pages. She has illustrated over 30 books for children. A former advertising illustrator, she is now a full-time freelance artist.

When Annie creates illustrations for a book, she pretends she is the main character, and the ideas flow from there. Her husband and their three children often act as inspirations for her work.

Annie and her family live by the ocean. Annie works in an attic that looks out over a beautiful large tree.